KU-781-737

GHOST TROUBLE, SNAKE TROUBLE

Imagine if a naughty ghost decided to haunt your house or if your grandfather brought home a python! That's what happens in these two lively stories set in north India.

Ruskin Bond lives in Mussoorie in the Himalayas and over the years he has heard and collected many Indian legends. He has also written many original stories of his own, set in India, including the Walker titles *Earthquake*, *Getting Granny's Glasses*, *Cricket for the Crocodile* and *Dust on the Mountain*. He is a former winner of the John Llewellyn Rhys Award for a first novel.

330023622X

More Walker Doubles

Ghost Trouble
Snake Trouble

RUSKIN BOND

Illustrated by
Barbara Walker

CLASS NO J823.9 BON
ITEM NO 330023622X
THE LIBRARY
MINSTER COLLEGE
RD OX2 9AT

WALKER BOOKS
LONDON

This story is for Mukesh
(Snake Trouble)

First published by Julia MacRae Books
as *Snake Trouble* (1990) and *Ghost Trouble* (1989)
This edition published 1992 by Walker Books Ltd
87 Vauxhall Walk, London SE11 5HJ

Text © 1989, 1990 Ruskin Bond
Illustrations © 1989, 1990 Barbara Walker
Cover illustration © 1992 Sue Heap

Printed and bound in Great Britain by
Richard Clay Ltd, Bungay, Suffolk

British Library Cataloguing in Publication Data
A catalogue record for this title is available
from the British Library.
ISBN 0-7445-2369-9

Ghost Trouble

Chapter 1

It was Grandfather who finally decided that we would have to move to another house.

And it was all because of a Pret, a mischievous north-Indian ghost, who had been making life difficult for everyone.

Prets usually live in peepal trees, and that's where our little ghost first had his home – in the branches of a massive old peepal tree which had grown through the compound wall and spread into our garden. Part of the tree was on our side of the wall, part on the other side, shading the main road. It gave the ghost a good view of the whole area.

For many years the Pret had lived there quite happily, without bothering anyone in our house. It did not bother me, either, and I spent a lot of time in the peepal tree. Sometimes I went there to escape the adults at home,

sometimes to watch the road and the people who passed by. The peepal tree was cool on a hot day, and the heart-shaped leaves were always revolving in the breeze. This constant movement of the leaves also helped to disguise the movements of the Pret, so that I never really knew exactly where he was sitting. But he paid no attention to me. The traffic on the road kept him fully occupied.

Sometimes, when a tonga was passing, he would jump down and frighten the pony, and as a result the little pony-cart would go rushing off in the wrong direction.

Sometimes he would get into the

engine of a car or a bus, which
would have a breakdown soon
afterwards.

And he liked to knock the sun-
helmets off the heads of sahibs or
officials, who would wonder how a
strong breeze had sprung up so

suddenly, only to die down just as quickly. Although this special kind of ghost could make himself felt, and sometimes heard, he was invisible to the human eye.

I was not invisible to the human eye, and often got the blame for some of the Pret's pranks. If bicycle-riders were struck by mango seeds or apricot stones, they would look up, see a small boy in the branches of the tree, and threaten me with terrible consequences. Drivers who went off after parking their cars in the shade would sometimes come back to find their tyres flat. My protests of innocence did not carry much weight. But

when I mentioned the Pret in the
tree, they would look uneasy, either
because they thought I must be
mad, or because they were afraid of
ghosts, especially Prets. They would
find other things to do and hurry
away.

At night no one walked beneath the peepal tree.

It was said that if you yawned beneath the tree, the Pret would jump down your throat and give you a pain. Our gardener, Chandu, who was always taking sick-leave, blamed the Pret for his tummy troubles. Once, when yawning, Chandu had forgotten to put his hand in front of his mouth, and the ghost had got in without any trouble.

Now Chandu spent most of his time lying on a string-bed in the courtyard of his small house. When Grandmother went to visit him, he would start groaning and holding

his sides, the pain was so bad; but
when she went away, he did not
fuss so much. He claimed that the
pain did not affect his appetite, and
he ate a normal diet, in fact a little
more than normal – the extra
amount was meant to keep the
ghost happy!

Chapter 2

"Well, it isn't our fault," said Grandfather, who had given permission to the Public Works Department to cut the tree, which had been on our land. They wanted to widen the road, and the tree and a bit of our wall were in the way. So both had to go.

Several people protested, including the Raja of Jinn, who lived across the road and who sometimes asked Grandfather over for a game of tennis.

"That peepal tree has been there

for hundreds of years," he said. "Who are we to cut it down?"

"*We*," said the Chief Engineer, "are the P.W.D."

And not even a ghost can prevail against the wishes of the Public Works Department.

They brought men with saws and axes, and first they lopped all the branches until the poor tree was quite naked. It must have been at this moment that the Pret moved out. Then they sawed away at the trunk until, finally, the great old peepal came crashing down on the road, bringing down the telephone wires and an electric pole in the process, and knocking a large gap

in the Raja's garden wall.

It took them three days to clear
the road, and during that time the
Chief Engineer swallowed a lot of
dust and tree-pollen. For months
afterwards he complained of a
choking feeling, although no doctor

could ever find anything in his throat.

"It's the Pret's doing," said the Raja knowingly. "They should never have cut that tree."

Deprived of his tree, the Pret decided that he would live in our house.

I first became aware of his presence when I was sitting on the verandah steps, reading a book. A tiny chuckling sound came from behind me. I looked round, but no one was to be seen. When I returned to my book, the chuckling started again. I paid no attention.

Then a shower of rose petals fell softly on to the pages of my open book. The Pret wanted me to know he was there!

"All right," I said. "So you've come to stay with us. Now let me read."

He went away then; but as a good Pret has to be bad in order to justify his existence, it was not long before he was up to all sorts of mischief.

He began by hiding Grandmother's spectacles.

"I'm sure I put them down on the dining-table," she grumbled.

A little later they were found balanced on the snout of a wild boar, whose stuffed and mounted

head adorned the verandah wall, a memento of Grandfather's hunting trips when he was young.

Naturally, I was at first blamed for this prank. But a day or two later, when the spectacles disappeared again, only to be found dangling from the bars of the parrot's cage, it was agreed that I was not to blame; for the parrot had once bitten off a piece of my finger, and I did not go near it any more.

The parrot was hanging upside down, trying to peer through one of the lenses. I don't know if they improved his vision, but what he saw certainly made him angry, because the pupils of his eyes went very small and he dug his beak into the spectacle frames, leaving them with a permanent dent. I caught them just before they fell to the floor.

But even without the help of the spectacles, it seemed that our parrot could see the Pret. He would keep turning this way and that, lunging out at unseen fingers, and protecting his tail from the tweaks of invisible hands. He had always refused to learn to talk, but now he became quite voluble and began to chatter in some unknown tongue, often screaming with rage and rolling his eyes in a frenzy.

"We'll have to give that parrot

away," said Grandmother. "He gets more bad-tempered by the day."

Grandfather was the next to be troubled.

He went into the garden one morning to find all his prize sweet-peas broken off and lying on the grass. Chandu thought the sparrows had destroyed the flowers, but we didn't think the birds could have finished off every single bloom just before sunrise.

"It must be the Pret," said Grandfather, and I agreed.

The Pret did not trouble me much, because he remembered me from his peepal-tree days and knew I resented the tree being cut as much as he did. But he liked to catch my attention, and he did this by chuckling and squeaking near me when I was alone, or whispering in my ear when I was with someone else. Gradually I began to make out the occasional word. He had started learning English!

Chapter 3

Uncle Benji, who came to stay with us for long periods when he had little else to do (which was most of the time), was soon to suffer.

He was a heavy sleeper, and once he'd gone to bed he hated being woken up. So when he came to breakfast looking bleary-eyed and miserable, we asked him if he was feeling all right.

"I couldn't sleep a wink last night," he complained. "Whenever I was about to fall asleep, the bedclothes would be pulled off the bed. I had to get up at least a dozen times to pick them off the floor." He stared suspiciously at me. "Where were *you* sleeping last night, young man?"

"In Grandfather's room," I said. "I've lent you *my* room."

"It's that ghost from the peepal tree," said Grandmother with a sigh.

"Ghost!" exclaimed Uncle Benji. "I didn't know the house was haunted."

"It is now," said Grandmother. "First my spectacles, then the sweet-peas, and now Benji's bedclothes! What will it be up to next, I wonder?"

We did not have to wonder for long.

There followed a series of minor disasters. Vases fell off tables, pictures fell from walls. Parrots' feathers turned up in the teapot, while the parrot himself let out indignant squawks and swearwords in the middle of the night. Windows which had been closed would be found open, and open windows closed.

Finally, Uncle Benji found a crow's nest in his bed, and on tossing it out of the window was attacked by two crows.

Then Aunt Ruby came to stay, and things quietened down for a time.

Did Aunt Ruby's powerful personality have an effect on the Pret, or was he just sizing her up?

"I think the Pret has taken a fancy to your aunt," said Grandfather mischievously. "He's behaving himself for a change."

This may have been true, because the parrot, who had picked up some of the English words being tried out by the Pret, now called out, "*Kiss, kiss*," whenever Aunt Ruby was in the room.

"What a charming bird," said Aunt Ruby.

"You can keep him if you like," said Grandmother.

One day Aunt Ruby came in to the house covered in rose petals.

"I don't know where they came from," she exclaimed. "I was sitting

in the garden, drying my hair,
when handfuls of petals came
showering down on me!"

"It likes you," said Grandfather.

"What likes me?"

"The ghost."

"What ghost?"

"The Pret. It came to live in the
house when the peepal tree was cut
down."

"What nonsense!" said Aunt Ruby.

"*Kiss, kiss!*" screamed the parrot.

"There aren't any ghosts, Prets or other kinds," said Aunt Ruby firmly.

"*Kiss, kiss!*" screeched the parrot again. Or was it the parrot? The sound seemed to be coming from the ceiling.

"I wish that parrot would shut up."

"It isn't the parrot," I said. "It's the Pret."

Aunt Ruby gave me a cuff over the ear and stormed out of the room.

But she had offended the Pret.

From being her admirer, he turned
into her enemy. Somehow her
toothpaste got switched with a tube
of Grandfather's shaving-cream.
When she appeared in the dining-
room, foaming at the mouth, we
ran for our lives, Uncle Benji
shouting that she'd got rabies.

Chapter 4

Two days later Aunt Ruby complained that she had been struck on the nose by a grapefruit, which had leapt mysteriously from the pantry shelf and hurled itself at her.

"If Ruby and Benji stay here much longer, they'll both have nervous breakdowns," said Grandfather thoughtfully.

"I thought they broke down long ago," I said.

"None of your cheek," snapped Aunt Ruby.

"He's in league with that Pret to try and get us out of here," said Uncle Benji.

"Don't listen to him – you can stay as long as you like," said Grandmother, who never turned away any of her numerous nephews, nieces, cousins or distant relatives.

The Pret, however, did not feel so hospitable, and the persecution of Aunt Ruby continued.

"When I looked in the mirror this morning," she complained bitterly, "I saw a little monster, with huge ears, bulging eyes, flaring nostrils and a toothless grin!"

"You don't look *that* bad, Aunt

Ruby," I said, trying to be nice.

"It was either you or that imp you call a Pret," said Aunt Ruby. "And if it's a ghost, then it's time we all moved to another house."

Uncle Benji had another idea.

"Let's drive the ghost out," he said. "I know a Sadhu who rids houses of evil spirits."

"But the Pret's not evil," I said. "Just mischievous."

Uncle Benji went off to the bazaar and came back a few hours later with a mysterious long-haired man who claimed to be a Sadhu — one who has given up all worldly goods, including most of his clothes.

He prowled about the house, and lighted incense in all the rooms, despite squawks of protest from the parrot. All the time he chanted various magic spells. He then collected a fee of thirty rupees, and

promised that we would not be
bothered again by the Pret.

As he was leaving, he was
suddenly blessed with a shower –
no, it was really a downpour – of
dead flowers, decaying leaves,
orange peel and banana skins. All
spells forgotten, he ran to the gate

and made for the safety of the bazaar.

Aunt Ruby declared that it had become impossible to sleep at night because of the devilish chuckling that came from beneath her pillow. She packed her bags and left.

Uncle Benji stayed on. He was still having trouble with his bedclothes, and he was beginning to talk to himself, which was a bad sign.

"Talking to the Pret, Uncle?" I asked innocently, when I caught him at it one day.

He gave me a threatening look.

"What did you say?" he demanded. "Would you mind repeating that?"

I thought it safer to please him. "Oh, didn't you hear me?" I said, *"Teaching the parrot, Uncle?"*

He glared at me, then walked off in a huff. If he did not leave it was because he was hoping Grandmother would lend him enough money to buy a motorcycle; but Grandmother said he ought to try earning a living first.

One day I found him on the drawing-room sofa, laughing like a madman. Even the parrot was so alarmed that it was silent, head lowered and curious. Uncle Benji was red in the face – literally red all over!

"What happened to your face, Uncle?" I asked.

He stopped laughing and gave me a long hard look. I realized that there had been no joy in his laughter.

"Who painted the wash-basin red without telling me?" he asked in a quavering voice.

As Uncle Benji looked really dangerous, I ran from the room.

"We'll have to move, I suppose," said Grandfather later. "Even if it's only for a couple of months. I'm worried about Benji. I've told him that I painted the wash-basin myself but forgot to tell him. He doesn't believe me. He thinks it's the Pret or the boy, or both of them! Benji needs a change. So do we. There's my brother's house at the other end of the town. He won't be using it for a few months. We'll move in next week."

And so, a few days and several disasters later, we began moving house.

Chapter 5

Two bullock-carts laden with
furniture and heavy luggage were
sent ahead. Uncle Benji went with
them. The roof of our old car was
piled high with bags and kitchen
utensils. Grandfather took the
wheel, I sat beside him, and
Granny sat in state at the back.

We set off and had gone some
way down the main road when
Grandfather started having trouble
with the steering-wheel. It appeared
to have got loose, and the car
began veering about on the road,

scattering cyclists, pedestrians, and
stray dogs, pigs and hens. A cow
refused to move, but we missed it
somehow, and then suddenly we
were off the road and making for a
low wall. Grandfather pressed his
foot down on the brake, but we only
went faster. "Watch out!" he
shouted.

It was the Raja of Jinn's garden
wall, made of single bricks, and the
car knocked it down quite easily
and went on through it, coming to a
stop on the Raja's lawn.

"Now look what you've done,"
said Grandmother.

"Well, we missed the flower-
beds," said Grandfather.

"Someone's been tinkering with the car. Our Pret, no doubt."

The Raja and two attendants came running towards us.

The Raja was a perfect gentleman, and when he saw that the driver was Grandfather, he beamed with pleasure.

"Delighted to see you, old chap!" he exclaimed. "Jolly decent of you to drop in. How about a game of tennis?"

"Sorry to have come in through the wall," apologized Grandfather.

"Don't mention it, old chap. The gate was closed, so what else could you do?"

Grandfather was as much of a

gentleman as the Raja, so he thought it only fair to join him in a game of tennis. Grandmother and I watched and drank lemonade. After the game, the Raja waved us good-bye and we drove back through the hole in the wall and out on to the road. There was nothing much wrong with the car.

We hadn't gone far when we heard a peculiar sound, as of someone chuckling and talking to himself. It came from the roof of the car.

"Is the parrot out there on the luggage-rack?" asked Grandfather.

"No," said Grandmother. "He went ahead with Uncle Benji."

Grandfather stopped the car, got out, and examined the roof.

"Nothing up there," he said, getting in again and starting the engine. "I thought I heard the parrot."

When we had gone a little further, the chuckling started again. A squeaky little voice began talking in English in the tones of the parrot.

"It's the Pret," whispered Grandmother. "What is he saying?"

The Pret's squeak grew louder. "Come on, come on!" he cried gleefully. "A new house! The same old friends! What fun we're going to have!"

Grandfather stopped the car. He backed into a driveway, turned round, and began driving back to our old house.

"What are you doing?" asked Grandmother.

"Going home," said Grandfather.

"And what about the Pret?"

"What about him? He's decided to live with us, so we'll have to make the best of it. You can't solve a problem by running away from it."

"All right," said Grandmother. "But what will we do about Benji?"

"It's up to him, isn't it? He'll be all right if he finds something to do."

Grandfather stopped the car in front of the verandah steps.

"I'm hungry," I said.

"It will have to be a picnic lunch," said Grandmother. "Almost everything was sent off on the bullock-carts."

As we got out of the car and climbed the verandah steps, we were greeted by showers of rose petals and sweet-scented jasmine.

"How lovely!" exclaimed Grandmother, smiling. "I think he likes us, after all."

SNAKE TROUBLE

Chapter 1

After retiring from the Indian Railways and settling in Dehra, Grandfather often made his days (and ours) more exciting by keeping unusual pets. He paid a snake-charmer in the bazaar twenty rupees for a young python. Then, to the delight of a curious group of boys and girls, he slung the python over his shoulder and brought it home.

I was with him at the time, and felt very proud walking beside Grandfather. He was popular in

Dehra, especially among the poorer
people, and everyone greeted him
politely without seeming to notice
the python. They were, in fact,
quite used to seeing him in the
company of strange creatures.

The first to see us arrive was Toto the monkey, who was swinging from a branch of the jack-fruit tree. One look at the python, ancient enemy of his race, and he fled into the house squealing with fright. Then our parrot, Popeye, who had his perch on the verandah, set up the most awful shrieking and whistling. His whistle was like that of a steam-engine. He had learnt to do this in earlier days, when we had lived near railway-stations.

The noise brought Grandmother to the verandah, where she nearly fainted at the sight of the python curled round Grandfather's neck.

Grandmother put up with most of

his pets, but she drew the line at reptiles. Even a sweet-tempered lizard made her blood run cold. There was little chance that she would allow a python in the house.

"It will strangle you to death!" she cried.

"Nonsense," said Grandfather. "He's only a young fellow."

"He'll soon get used to us," I added, by way of support.

"He might, indeed," said Grandmother, "but I have no intention of getting used to him. And your Aunt Ruby is coming to stay with us tomorrow. She'll leave the minute she knows there's a snake in the house."

"Well, perhaps we should show it to her first thing," said Grandfather, who found Aunt Ruby rather tiresome.

"Get rid of it right away," said Grandmother.

"I can't let it loose in the garden. It might find its way into the chicken shed, and then where will we be?"

"Minus a few chickens," I said reasonably, but this only made Grandmother more determined to get rid of the python.

"Lock that awful thing in the bathroom," she said. "Go and find the man you bought it from, and get him to come here and collect it! He can keep the money you gave him."

Grandfather and I took the snake into the bathroom and placed it in an empty tub. Looking a bit crestfallen, he said, "Perhaps your grandmother is right. I'm not worried about Aunt Ruby, but we don't want the python to get hold of Toto or Popeye."

We hurried off to the bazaar in search of the snake-charmer but hadn't gone far when we found several snake-charmers looking for us. They had heard that Grandfather was buying snakes, and they had brought with them snakes of various sizes and descriptions.

"No, no!" protested Grandfather.

"We don't want more snakes. We want to return the one we bought."

But the man who had sold it to us had, apparently, returned to his village in the jungle, looking for another python for Grandfather; and the other snake-charmers were not interested in buying, only in selling. In order to shake them off, we had to return home by a roundabout route, climbing a wall and cutting through an orchard. We found Grandmother pacing up and down the verandah. One look at our faces and she knew we had failed to get rid of the snake.

"All right," said Grandmother. "Just take it away yourselves and

see that it doesn't come back."

"We'll get rid of it, Grandmother," I said confidently. "Don't you worry."

Grandfather opened the bathroom door and stepped into the room. I was close behind him. We couldn't see the python anywhere.

"He's gone," announced Grandfather.

"We left the window open," I said.

"Deliberately, no doubt," said Grandmother. "But it couldn't have gone far. You'll have to search the grounds, Ranji."

A careful search was made of the house, the roof, the kitchen, the garden and the chicken shed, but there was no sign of the python.

"He must have gone over the garden wall," Grandfather said cheerfully. "He'll be well away by now!"

The python did not reappear, and when Aunt Ruby arrived with enough luggage to show that she had come for a long visit, there was only the parrot to greet her with a series of long, ear-splitting whistles.

Chapter 2

For a couple of days Grandfather and I were a little worried that the python might make a sudden reappearance, but when he didn't show up again we felt he had gone for good. Aunt Ruby had to put up with Toto the monkey making faces at her, something I did only when she wasn't looking; and she complained that Popeye shrieked loudest when she was in the room; but she was used to them, and knew she would have to bear with them if she was going to stay with us.

And then, one evening, we were startled by a scream from the garden.

Seconds later Aunt Ruby came flying up the verandah steps, gasping, "In the guava tree! I was reaching for a guava when I saw it staring at me. The look in its eyes! As though it would eat me alive –"

"Calm down, dear," urged Grandmother, sprinkling rose-water over my aunt. "Tell us, what *did* you see?"

"A snake!" sobbed Aunt Ruby. "A great boa constrictor in the guava tree. Its eyes were terrible, and it looked at me in such a *queer* way."

"Trying to tempt you with a guava, no doubt," said Grandfather, turning away to hide his smile. He gave me a look full of meaning, and I hurried out into the garden. But when I got to the guava tree, the python (if it had been the python) had gone.

"Aunt Ruby must have frightened it off," I told Grandfather.

"I'm not surprised," he said. "But it will be back, Ranji. I think it's taken a fancy to your aunt."

Sure enough, the python began to make brief but frequent appearances, usually turning up in the most unexpected places.

One morning I found him curled up on a dressing-table, gazing at his own reflection in the mirror. I

went for Grandfather, but by the time we returned the python had moved on.

He was seen again in the garden, and one day I spotted him climbing the iron ladder to the roof. I set off after him, and was soon up the ladder, which I had climbed up many times. I arrived on the flat roof just in time to see the snake disappearing down a drain-pipe. The end of his tail was visible for a few moments and then that too disappeared.

"I think he lives in the drain-pipe," I told Grandfather.

"Where does it get its food?" asked Grandmother.

"Probably lives on those field rats that used to be such a nuisance. Remember, they lived in the drain-pipes, too."

"Hmm..." Grandmother looked thoughtful. "A snake has its uses. Well, as long as it keeps to the roof and prefers rats to chickens ..."

But the python did not confine itself to the roof. Piercing shrieks from Aunt Ruby had us all rushing to her room. There was the python on *her* dressing-table, apparently admiring himself in the mirror.

"All the attention he's been getting has probably made him conceited," said Grandfather, picking up the python to the accompaniment of further shrieks from Aunt Ruby. "Would you like to hold him for a minute, Ruby? He seems to have taken a fancy to you."

Aunt Ruby ran from the room and onto the verandah, where she was greeted with whistles of derision from Popeye the parrot. Poor Aunt Ruby! She cut short her stay by a week and returned to Lucknow, where she was a schoolteacher. She said she felt safer in her school than she did in our house.

Chapter 3

Having seen Grandfather handle the python with such ease and confidence, I decided I would do likewise. So the next time I saw the snake climbing the ladder to the roof, I climbed up alongside him. He stopped, and I stopped too. I put out my hand, and he slid over my arm and up to my shoulder. As I did not want him coiling round my neck, I gripped him with both hands and carried him down to the garden. He didn't seem to mind.

The snake felt rather cold and

slippery and at first he gave me
goose pimples. But I soon got used
to him, and he must have liked the
way I handled him, because when I
set him down he wanted to climb up
my leg. As I had other things to do,
I dropped him in a large empty
basket that had been left out in the

garden. He stared out at me with unblinking, expressionless eyes. There was no way of knowing what he was thinking, if indeed he thought at all.

I went off for a bicycle ride, and when I returned, found Grandmother picking guavas and dropping them into the basket. The python must have gone elsewhere.

When the basket was full, Grandmother said, "Will you take these over to Major Malik? It's his birthday and I want to give him a nice surprise."

I fixed the basket on the carrier of my cycle and pedalled off to Major Malik's house at the end of the

road. The Major met me on the
steps of his house.

"And what has your kind granny
sent me today, Ranji?" he asked.

"A surprise for your Happy
Birthday, sir," I said, and put the
basket down in front of him.

The python, who had been buried beneath all the guavas, chose this moment to wake up and stand straight up to a height of several feet. Guavas tumbled all over the place. The Major uttered an oath and dashed indoors.

I pushed the python back into the basket, picked it up, mounted the bicycle, and rode out of the gate in record time. And it was as well that I did so, because Major Malik came charging out of the house armed with a double-barrelled shotgun, which he was waving all over the place.

"Did you deliver the guavas?" asked Grandmother when I got back.

"I delivered them," I said truthfully.

"And was he pleased?"

"He's going to write and thank you," I said.

And he did.

'*Thank you for the lovely surprise,*' he wrote. '*Obviously you could not have known that my doctor had advised me against any undue excitement. My blood-pressure has been rather high. The sight of your grandson does not improve it. All the same, it's the thought that matters and I take it all in good humour ...*'

"What a strange letter," said Grandmother. "He must be ill, poor man. Are guavas bad for blood-pressure?"

"Not by themselves, they aren't," said Grandfather, who had an inkling of what had happened. "But together with other things they can be a bit upsetting."

Chapter 4

Just when all of us, including Grandmother, were getting used to having the python about the house and grounds, it was decided that we would be going to Lucknow for a few months.

Lucknow was a large city, about three hundred miles from Dehra. Aunt Ruby lived and worked there. We would be staying with her, and so of course we couldn't take any pythons, monkeys or other unusual pets with us.

"What about Popeye?" I asked.

"Popeye isn't a pet," said Grandmother. "He's one of us. He comes too."

And so the Dehra railway platform was thrown into confusion by the shrieks and whistles of our parrot, who could imitate both the guard's whistle and the whistle of a train. People dashed into their compartments, thinking the train was about to leave, only to realise

that the guard hadn't blown his whistle after all. When they got down, Popeye would let out another shrill whistle, which sent everyone rushing for the train again. This happened several times until the guard actually blew his whistle. Then nobody bothered to get on, and several passengers were left behind.

"Can't you gag that parrot?" asked Grandfather, as the train moved out of the station and picked up speed.

"I'll do nothing of the sort," said Grandmother. "I've bought a ticket for him, and he's entitled to enjoy the journey as much as anyone."

Whenever we stopped at a
station, Popeye objected to fruit
sellers and other people poking their
heads in at the windows. Before the
journey was over, he had nipped
two fingers and a nose, and
tweaked a ticket-inspector's ear.

It was to be a night journey, and
presently Grandmother covered

herself with a blanket and stretched herself out on the berth. "It's been a tiring day. I think I'll go to sleep," she said.

"Aren't we going to eat anything?" I asked.

"I'm not hungry – I had something before we left the house. You two help yourselves from the picnic hamper."

Grandmother dozed off, and even Popeye started nodding, lulled to sleep by the clackety-clack of the wheels and the steady puffing of the steam-engine.

"Well, I'm hungry," I said. "What did Granny make for us?"

"Stuffed samosas, omelettes, and

a tandoori chicken. It's all in the hamper under the berth."

I tugged at the cane box and dragged it into the middle of the compartment. The straps were loosely tied. No sooner had I undone them than the lid flew open, and I let out a gasp of surprise.

In the hamper was a python, curled up contentedly. There was no sign of our dinner.

"It's a python," I said. "And it's finished all our dinner."

"Nonsense," said Grandfather, joining me near the hamper. "Pythons won't eat omelettes and samosas. They like their food alive! Why, this isn't our hamper. The one with our food in it must have been left behind! Wasn't it Major Malik who helped us with our luggage? I think he's got his own back on us by changing the hamper!"

Grandfather snapped the hamper shut and pushed it back beneath the berth.

"Don't let Grandmother see him," he said. "She might think we brought him along on purpose."

"Well, I'm hungry," I complained.

"Wait till we get to the next station, then we can buy some pakoras. Meanwhile, try some of Popeye's green chillies."

"No thanks," I said. "You have them, Grandad."

And Grandfather, who could eat chillies plain, popped a couple into his mouth and munched away contentedly.

★

A little after midnight there was a great clamour at the end of the

corridor. Popeye made complaining
squawks, and Grandfather and I
got up to see what was wrong.

Suddenly there were cries of
"Snake, snake!"

I looked under the berth. The
hamper was open.

"The python's out," I said, and
Grandfather dashed out of the
compartment in his pyjamas. I was
close behind.

About a dozen passengers were bunched together outside the washroom door.

"Anything wrong?" asked Grandfather casually.

"We can't get into the toilet," said someone. "There's a huge snake inside."

"Let me take a look," said Grandfather. "I know all about snakes."

The passengers made way, and Grandfather and I entered the washroom together, but there was no sign of the python.

"He must have got out through the ventilator," said Grandfather. "By now he'll be in another compartment!" Emerging from the washroom, he told the assembled passengers "It's gone! Nothing to worry about. Just a harmless young python."

When we got back to our compartment, Grandmother was sitting up on her berth.

"I *knew* you'd do something foolish behind my back," she scolded. "You told me you'd left that creature behind, and all the time it was with us on the train."

Grandfather tried to explain that we had nothing to do with it, that this python had been smuggled onto the train by Major Malik, but Grandmother was unconvinced.

"Anyway, it's gone," said Grandfather. "It must have fallen out of the washroom window. We're over a hundred miles from Dehra, so you'll never see it again."

Even as he spoke, the train slowed down and lurched to a grinding halt.

"No station here," said Grandfather, putting his head out of the window.

Someone came rushing along the embankment, waving his arms and shouting.

"I do believe it's the stoker," said Grandfather. "I'd better go and see what's wrong."

"I'm coming too," I said, and together we hurried along the

length of the stationary train until we reached the engine.

"What's up?" called Grandfather. "Anything I can do to help? I know all about engines."

But the engine-driver was speechless. And who could blame him? The python had curled itself about his legs, and the driver was too petrified to move.

"Just leave it to us," said Grandfather, and, dragging the python off the driver, he dumped the snake in my arms. The engine-driver sank down on the floor, pale and trembling.

"I think I'd better drive the engine," said Grandfather. "We

don't want to be late getting into
Lucknow. Your aunt will be
expecting us!" And before the
astonished driver could protest,
Grandfather had released the
brakes and set the engine in motion.

"We've left the stoker behind," I
said.

"Never mind. You can shovel the coal."

Only too glad to help Grandfather drive an engine, I dropped the python in the driver's lap, and started shovelling coal. The engine picked up speed and we were soon rushing through the darkness, sparks flying skywards and the steam-whistle shrieking almost without pause.

"You're going too fast!" cried the driver.

"Making up for lost time," said Grandfather. "Why did the stoker run away?"

"He went for the guard. You've left them both behind!"

Chapter 5

Early next morning the train
steamed safely into Lucknow.
Explanations were in order, but as
the Lucknow station-master was an
old friend of Grandfather's, all was
well. We had arrived twenty
minutes early, and while
Grandfather went off to have a cup
of tea with the engine-driver and
the station-master, I returned the
python to the hamper and helped
Grandmother with the luggage.
Popeye stayed perched on
Grandmother's shoulder, eyeing the

busy platform with deep distrust.
He was the first to see Aunt Ruby
striding down the platform, and let
out a warning whistle.

Aunt Ruby, a lover of good food,
immediately spotted the picnic
hamper, picked it up and said, "It's
quite heavy. You must have kept
something for me! I'll carry it out to
the taxi."

'We hardly ate anything," I said.

"It seems ages since I tasted something cooked by your granny." And after that there was no getting the hamper away from Aunt Ruby.

Glancing at it, I thought I saw the lid bulging, but I had tied it down quite firmly this time and there was little likelihood of its suddenly bursting open.

Grandfather joined us outside the station and we were soon settled inside the taxi. Aunt Ruby gave instructions to the driver and we shot off in a cloud of dust.

"I'm dying to see what's in the hamper," said Aunt Ruby. "Can't I take just a little peek?"

"Not now," said Grandfather.
"First let's enjoy the breakfast
you've got waiting for us."

Popeye, perched proudly on
Grandmother's shoulder, kept one
suspicious eye on the quivering
hamper.

When we got to Aunt Ruby's
house, we found breakfast laid out
on the dining-table.

"It isn't much," said Aunt Ruby. "But we'll supplement it with what you've brought in the hamper."

Placing the hamper on the table, she lifted the lid and peered inside. And promptly fainted.

*

Grandfather picked up the python, took it into the garden, and draped it over a branch of a pomegranate tree.

When Aunt Ruby recovered, she insisted that she had seen a huge snake in the picnic hamper. We showed her the empty basket.

"You're seeing things," said

Grandfather. "You've been working too hard."

"Teaching is a very tiring job," I said solemnly.

Grandmother said nothing. But Popeye broke into loud squawks and whistles, and soon everyone, including a slightly hysterical Aunt Ruby, was doubled up with laughter.

But the snake must have tired of the joke because we never saw it again!

MORE WALKER PAPERBACKS
For You to Enjoy

☐ 0-7445-2305-2   *Dockside School Stories*
by Bernard Ashley   £2.99

☐ 0-7445-3014-8   *More Stories from
Dockside School*
by Bernard Ashley   £2.99

☐ 0-7445-2313-3   *The Dream Camel and
the Dazzling Cat*
by Diana Hendry   £2.99

☐ 0-7445-2303-6   *Hannah and Darjeeling*
by Diana Hendry   £2.99

☐ 0-7445-2314-1   *Fay Cow and the Honey
Machine*
by Peter Hunt   £2.99

☐ 0-7445-2302-8   *Smudge*
by Alison Morgan   £2.99

**Walker Paperbacks are available from most booksellers. They are also available
by post: just tick the titles you want, fill in the form below and send it to
Walker Books Ltd, PO Box 11, Falmouth, Cornwall TR10 9EN.**

Please send a cheque or postal order and allow the following for postage and packing:
UK and BFPO Customers – £1.00 for first book, plus 50p for the second book and
plus 30p for each additional book to a maximum charge of £3.00.
Overseas and Eire Customers – £2.00 for first book, plus £1.00 for the second book and
plus 50p per copy for each additional book.
Prices are correct at time of going to press, but are subject to change without notice.

Name _____

Address _____